A WINE LOVERS GUIDE TO PARENTING

By

Danielle Sloane Frank

Published by
Hybrid Global Publishing
333 E 14th Street #3C New York, NY 10003
Copyright © 2025 by Danielle Sloane Frank

Frank, Danielle Sloane
A Wine Lovers Guide to Parenting
Hardcover ISBN: 978-1-967598-06-9
E-book ISBN : 978-1-967598-07-6

Cover design by: Joe Potter
Copyediting by: Wendy Pecharsky
Interior design by: Amit Dey
Author photo by: Frank, Danielle Sloane
Illustrations by: Eris Aruman

Grab my book along with a nice glass of red or white wine
relax in a chair, ideally one that will recline
Allow yourself to heed my advice & your kids will turn out fine
Because you don't want your kid to end up as a bad grape on the **vine**
And while raising a kid there are no guarantees they'll turn out divine
But at least you can try and have some fun and learn a thing or two about wine.

*Grape **Vine** – any of numerous woody vines of genus Vitis bearing clusters of edible berries.*

LESSON 1:

I DRINK WINE, I DON'T LISTEN TO WHINE!

If you let your kids always whine to get their way
They'll continue to behave like that every single day
Stomp their feet and not listen to what you want to say
They'll be unruly, spoiled brats all to your dismay

Don't let them get what they want & throw a hissy fit
Because then they may just turn into a little shit

Once they've become spoiled rotten brats,
They think they run the show and there's no turning back

They'll continue that behavior because it's worked for them so far
Sure it's easy to give in now for things like a candy bar
But just wait until they're 17 and whining for a new car

Vinous – *The direct meaning is "like or related to wine," but to use it to describe a wine is to say "well, I can't find any flaws, but I can't find anything outstanding either. It just tastes like wine!"*

Vinous – *"of resembling or containing wine"*

So pour yourself a glass
And teach your kids some class
To ensure your kid doesn't turn into an ass

Though you want to give in to shut them up, it's best now to cut your loss
Do it while they are young & make sure they know it's you who is the boss

Impress that you won't put up with whining on any day
They will quickly learn that if they whine, they WON'T get their way

Let's face it, hearing a kid carry on and whine is not too cute
Do you really want a child that people want to put on mute?

When they whine, you simply can't say yes
When they're behaving well, that's when you can acquiesce
For that's the recipe for behavioral success
Cause you want to raise a child that will always impress
Not one that "tastes like whine," or **Vinous**

MUCH LIKE A FINE WINE, A KID NEEDS TO BREATHE

You need to let your kids breathe...how else will they grow?
If you're shielding them from life's downs, how will they know
the lessons we're meant to learn that life tends to show
It helps for them to learn to get up on their own when they feel so low
Because learning from their mistakes will help them to reap the seeds that you sow

If you don't let them ***aerate***
Who knows what you might create

Your job is to raise them for independence, to one day be on their own
Because you can't always solve their problems and wipe their ass when they are grown

---

Breathing *– allowing wine to come in contact with air to open and improve the flavors*

Aerate *- To allow a wine to "breathe" by exposing it to oxygen. Aerating a wine helps it to mellow and develop its full flavors, especially with red wines. Decanting is a way to aerate wine.*

Bordeaux *– A red or white wine produced in the region around Bordeaux, France*

Don't coddle your kid because then how will they learn
When playing with others, they need to take their turn
Or when they're older & working, skills needed to earn

Let them grow. Don't be too overbearing and baby them too much
You can't always be there, acting as a crutch

They need to fall in order to learn how to get back up on their feet
They need to understand being a good loser, when faced with defeat

They need to know life's about misses in order to appreciate when there's a hit
They should know there WILL be bumps in the road, but you cannot ever quit

You can teach them that bumps in the road are going to be okay
Don't hide behind them but handle them in a mature, problem solving way
You just brush yourself off and dust the urge to fall apart away
The most important part to this, is the lesson you takeaway

In the end, you are going to have to let them make a mistake
Even though watching them fall (not literally), makes your heart ache

The best lesson is don't cry over spilled wine (I mean milk), learn from it and grow
That will make them a fine individual, like a nice bottle of **Bordeaux**

LESSON 3:

YOU DON'T WANT YOUR KIDS TO FERMENT

Manners, manners, manners are the key to it all
These lessons need to start even when they are small
Teach them this from day one, before they start to crawl

You don't want your kid to be the sour grape in the bunch
And turn into a spoiled brat that kids want to punch

When they start talking, make sure they know thank you and please
And to always say bless you, when they hear someone sneeze

Please and thank you are an absolute must
Without that, your child's a total bust

---

ferment - *turning sugar into alcohol*

Harsh - *A harsh wine is overly astringent, due to exceptionally high levels of acid or tannins and alcohol. A wine that is harsh will taste rough, and while it is not entirely unpleasant, neither is it enjoyable. Occasionally, aging will help soften a harsh wine, but not necessarily. Often the duration of time required to decrease the harshness in the wine will negatively impact other factors of the wine. A harsh wine is similar to a hard wine, but harshness & extreme harshness is always considered a flaw.*

There's nothing worse than a child who has behavior that is crude
Cause it'll continue as they're older and become someone who's rude
People don't take kindly to & aren't nice to those with attitude
Because it's very off putting and puts others in a bad mood
Often times causing confrontation & leads to a nasty feud
Wanting to put a little bit of poison in your child's food
Is that really how you want your kids to be viewed?
Wouldn't you prefer that they are someone who's wooed?

Without manners, they'll ferment & turn into someone **harsh** & biting
They may turn into a kid who's rude, obnoxious and always fighting

Teach your kid some manners & to have some heart & soul
Without that, your kid may well turn into an a**hole

LESSON 4:

NOSE THE WINE TO MAKE SURE IT SMELLS FINE

When people *"nose"* your child, you want them to smell fresh and *clean*
Their skin with no dirt, the clothes not stained and their hair with a sheen
Because, unfortunately, other kids can be very cruel & mean

They say you can't judge a book by it's a cover, but sadly kids do
They will tease a child if his clothes look dirty and not brand new
Or if he has not showered and smells a little like Doo-doo

Nose (Aroma) - The nose of a wine can be one of the most enticing wine characteristics. Even before tasting the wine, you can be swept away by a beautiful bouquet of aromas that entice you to take a sip. Swirl the wine gently in the glass to aerate it and volatilize the aromatic compounds, making them easier to smell.

Clean - In wine tasting this term refers to wines that do not have any noticeable unpleasant or out-of-the-ordinary odors or flavors

Bouquet - Near synonym for "aroma," bouquet is a tasting term used to describe the complex <u>aromas</u> of an aged wine.

Cabernet Sauvignon – A red wine grape that is dominant in the French Bordeaux region and found in about every other region because it is so easy to grow. The result of a marriage between the Cabernet Franc and Sauvignon Blanc grapes, it is high in tannins, allowing it to age well. Of course, these tannins will soften over the aging time. Commonly brings to mind black currant and cedar.

Chardonnay - Originally from the French Burgundy and Champagne regions, this well-known white wine grape is now grown all over the world. The grape absorbs oak well and its taste will change from crisp and steel to butter and vanilla as a result of oak barreling. Regardless, the full body, rich flavor, and smooth finish that distinguish a Chardonnay will remain. It is best served cool and complements seafood well.

No one likes someone with a personality that's dour
But what is even worse than that is when someone smells sour
And is in desperate need of a bubble bath or shower

So ensure your child is on the right path
and you are frequently giving them a bath

Make sure that you notice and take special care
To ensure your child is combing their hair
Doing a good job to wipe their derriere,
picking out clean clothes & not stained ones to wear
Because you don't want other people to stare

In the end, you don't want someone to say your kid's a little shit
Not from behavior (like Lesson 1) cause they are throwing a fit
But because there's an awful smell coming from beneath their armpit

You want to hear "your baby is such a mensch"
Not, "ew, gross, who is that kid with the bad stench?"

You want your kid to have a nice **_bouquet_**
Much like a nice, full-bodied **Cabernet**,
Not like a bottle of cheap **_Chardonnay_**

DON'T LET YOUR CHILD LEAVE A BITTER TASTE IN YOUR MOUTH?

There is nothing worse than a kid who talks back
When I hear that from kids, I'm taken aback
It makes you the parent, look like a sad sack

Mouth-feel *how a wine feels in one's mouth – (eg. Rough, smooth, velvety, furry)*

Mouth (Flavor) *- The wine characteristic that culminates the wine tasting experience. Is it powerful or intense or is it slow to build or even flabby & lacking spirit? Is the* **mouthfeel** *rough and angular or smooth and seductive? Silky or velvety? Finally, the finish, the aftertaste of the wine that lingers in your mouth after you swallow or spit. Does it linger beautifully on your palate, enticing you to take another sip or does it cut off short, or even worse does it leave a strange, bitter or otherwise unsavory flavor in your mouth?*

Acidity *- The tart taste in wines. When there is too much acidity the wine can taste sour*

Bite *in a wine is defined as the rough, stinging sensation felt on the front of your tongue while drinking a sharp or astringent wine. Wines that have bite have heavy amounts of either acid or tannins.*

Aftertaste *-The taste that stays in your mouth after swallowing the wine. It should be pleasant and in fine wines it should last a long time after the wine is gone.*

Sauternes *is a* <u>French</u> <u>sweet wine</u> *from the Sauternes region of the* <u>Graves</u> *section in* <u>Bordeaux</u>. *Sauternes is made from* <u>Sémillon</u>, <u>Sauvignon Blanc</u>, *and* <u>Muscadelle grapes</u>

Astringent-*An astringent wine is a dry, bitter wine that creates a tight sensation in your mouth, often causing you to pucker. An overabundance of tannins causes a wine to taste astringent. Young red wines are especially susceptible to being astringent because the high levels of tannins that are there to help the wine age well, but have not had time to saturate and settle.*

And people want to give you some major flack
And even worse, wanna give your kid a nice smack
So don't let your kid get completely off track
If they mouth off, don't let the discipline lack

Don't let your child speak to you with a fresh mouth
Teach proper etiquette like they do in the south

There's nothing worse than seeing a child who's rude
Always walking around with a bad attitude

It's really not cute when you hear someone so young
So disrespectful and speaking with a sharp tongue

or when the things they say have an **acidic bite**
Acting rude & ill-mannered is never alright

If the things they say leave a bad **Aftertaste**
Those around you will surely want to lambaste
And you, as a parent, will feel disgraced

You want the way they speak to sound sweet like a song
Not a science project that's gone horribly wrong

A child who's fresh causes people around to show some concern
As to why you're allowing that behavior and not being stern
The words that come from your kid's mouth should be sweet like a fine **sauternes** (soh-turn)
Not like a cheap, young red wine that is **astringent** and tends to burn

LESSON 6:

"DECANT" LET THEM RUN YOU

It is vital, early on you need to set the tone
That you make the rules, no matter how much they moan
They need to know that they're not the boss of you
It's not they who gets to tell you what to do

<u>Decanting</u> *a wine is the process of pouring wine from the bottle into a glass decanter, in order to separate the* **sediment** *from the wine*

Sediment *- This describes the particles that sometimes occur in a bottle of wine. In young wines, sediment is a result of a weak filtering process during production and is described as making the wine cloudy or hazy. In old wines, sediment is a result of the tannins and dyes separating from the liquid and is often used in the form "thrown sediment."*

Zin *– (short for Zinfandel) When you think of this grape, you probably think a blush or white wine, and possibly not very highly. But the Zinfandel grape is a red grape, and it is now almost exclusively found in California. Red Zinfandels make a deep, alcoholic wine with a flavor that range from fruity to spicy flavor. White Zinfandels are actually a blush wine, with a very sweet and fruity flavor.*

Robust *– Full-bodied, powerful, heady*

Racking *- An important step in wine making. The transfer of the young wine from one barrel, where it has thrown some sediment, to a new barrel, leaving the sediment behind. Not only does this help to clarify the wine, it is an opportunity for the wine to come into contact with air. A certain amount of oxygen is required at this stage of a wine's development, in order to produce necessary aromas (secondary aromas). Racking must be conducted carefully, as too much oxygen will be more harmful than beneficial for the wine. Heavy red wines may be racked 3 or four times. Lighter reds and whites may only be racked once or twice.*

Like a decanter separates the **sediment** from the wine
You need to separate bad behavior so they turn out fine
There are definitive rules that you need to clearly define
Which will serve the purpose of separating you from the whine

Don't let your kids become totally whack
You need to let the kids properly **rack**

Letting your kids walk all over you doesn't teach proper values
It will be a never-ending fight that you will constantly lose
If you let the role of disciplinarian be in their shoes

Set the boundaries early on is something I recommend
Know there's a time & place to be a parent vs their friend

Disciplining your children is an absolute must
To ensure they're well-mannered and not overly **robust**

I know it can be hard because we all want to play good cop
But if you let them run over you, it will never stop

Sure, you want your kids to think that you are cool
But really you don't want to bc played a fool

Because once you let them run all over you
That is something that you both will get used to
It also doesn't help as they're older, too

They need to know deference to the teachers in their class
Teachers don't favor kids who act like a smartass

And when they are working at a high powered job
They won't last long if they act like a spoiled snob

Your children need to understand
That you are the one in command
And respect is what you demand

If you see bad behavior, it's something you must correct
You have to be the boss, make sure your message is direct
To instill in them proper values & teach them respect

Leave the **sediment** of their bad behavior behind
You helming the ship only helps to teach them to be kind

They don't call it tough love for nothing, but it will save your day
YOU need to rule the roost, don't let it get the other way
Setting the tone early will make disciplining later on child's play
And less likely your child be someone from which you want to get away!

In order to win, it's imperative to discipline
Then you can sit back and enjoy a nice bottle of **Zin**

You must not let your kids run amok
Or they'll turn into a little fuck

LESSON 7:

IS YOUR KID A MULLED WINE?

An extremely important fact of life that you must understand
Is bullying amongst kids has gotten completely out of hand

Bullying is a major problem amongst the youth today
Affects on the recipient sometimes never goes away

The impact on a child can completely affect their life
Making them insecure & depressed, causing them constant strife

---

Mulled Wine - *Wine that is spiced, heated, and served as a punch. Typically made from red wine (Cabernet, Zinfandel or **Merlot**) & various combinations of nutmeg, cloves, cinnamon, sugar & orange zest & served with a slice of orange or lemon.*

Merlot - *The classic Merlot grape originated from the Bordeaux region of France. It typically produces a soft, medium-bodied red wine with juicy fruit flavors. Fairly versatile when it comes to food pairing options. Poultry, red meat, pork, pastas, salads - Merlot can handle them all well.*

Rough - *A wine tasting term for a wine that is astringent and tannic out of balance. Mostly a term for young wines. Rough wines rarely soften enough with age to be really enjoyable. By the time the roughness has gone, so has all of the fruit.*

You need to know if your kid's 'packing a punch' to others at school
Are they making fun of the other kids and acting very cruel?

To the other kids are they acting real tough
Pushing and shoving and being **_rough_**

Are they considered a bully and perceived as mean?
If so, you make sure that you are aware of this scene
And it is imperative that you get in between
Stop this before it persists as they become a teen

You make sure your child knows that you will not tolerate
Any kind of conduct that is mean, rude and displays hate

We all want to imagine our kids as the perfect little star
But it's your job as a parent to be know who your kids really are
Are they sweet as pie when they're with you then a trouble when they're far?

This is very important so heed my advice
So pay attention & teach them to be nice
Not a **mulled wine** that is heated with some spice

Ensure your child is soft, even-bodied like a **Merlot**
Not rough and tough that others want to deal them a nasty blow

Recipe for Mulled Wine

- One bottle (750 mL) of red wine (suggestions: Cabernet Sauvignon, Zinfandel, Merlot)
- One peeled and sliced orange (keep peel to add zest to taste into cooking pot)
- 1/4 cup of brandy
- 8-10 cloves
- 2/3 cup honey or sugar
- 3 cinnamon sticks
- 1 tsp fresh or 2 tsp ground ginger (allspice can be substituted)
- Serves 4-6

Combine all ingredients in either a large pot or a slow cooker. Gently warm the ingredients on low to medium heat (avoid boiling), for 20-25 minutes. Stir occasionally to make sure that the honey or sugar has completely dissolved. When the wine is steaming and the ingredients have been well blended it is ready to serve. Ladle the mulled wine into mugs (leave seasonings behind). Garnish with a lemon or orange slice.

L E S S O N 8 :

TRY AND GIVE YOUR CHILD A NICE *PUNT*

You want your child to have **depth**, be worldly & well-rounded
Having an understanding of the world keeps them grounded

You do not want your child to be shielded and blinded
They should accept other people & be open-minded

It also helps to combat prejudice, because then they'll take kindly to
others that may look differently or speak another language than they do

---

Punt - *The indentation found in the base of a wine bottle. Punt depth is often thought to be related to wine quality, with better quality wines having a deeper punt.*

Depth, deep - *A tasting term referring to a wine that fills the mouth with an intense flavour.*

Pinot Noir – *red wine grape; grown especially in California for making wines resembling those from Burgundy, France. Pinot Noir tends to be high in acid, and low in tannin, which makes it easier to enjoy in its youth, and one of the best wines to enjoy with food. Pinot Noir is a very hard grape to grow, and a very hard wine to make.*

Vin – *French for wine*

They should have a broad aspect of human life & world view
And they will get that, the more that you can expose them to

You don't have to be wealthy & on a plane to travel all around
You can educate them on different cultures even being home bound

Read to them about all the types of people in the world there are to meet
Expose them to different foods when you are home or when you go out to eat

Ensure you read to them a wide array of books
Of many different cultures & how they may dress & have diverse looks

Whether someone is agnostic or pious
It is not for others to have bias

They should know it's not about the color of someone's skin
What's most important is being a good person within
What is Vino in Italy, Wein is in Berlin
In the U.S., we say wine but in France they say **Vin**

No one language is better than the other
And not one race is better than another

Not being exposed to different walks of life
Can make somebody ignorant & cause strife

With those around them that might not look the same
And someone that is hateful is quite a shame

Teach them that not one culture or race is right or wrong
We all share this planet, it's crucial we get along

Show that people are different in so many ways
Just like **Pinot Noirs** are different from Cabernets

It doesn't mean that a Cab is better than a Pinot
Or that both pale in comparison to a fine Bordeaux

They are all great in their own way & equally able
To all live in harmony on a dining room table

Without depth and worldliness, your child will not have a good punt
And could possibly turn into a complete & total..........
Ignorant, hateful kid....what? What did you think I was going to say there?

LOOKING AT LIFE THROUGH ROSE COLORED (WINE) GLASSES

The saying 'looking through **rose**-colored glasses' is being optimistic about things in life
Cause things in life can go wrong regardless, but being negative can add additional strife

When you are someone that views the glass half empty
You exhibit nothing but negativity
And that is quite simply no way to want to be
And can lead to a life that's very unhappy
Because the shining light, you simply cannot see

Teach your child to be optimistic, positive and bright
To see at the end of the tunnel, you can always find light
It doesn't always mean that everything will always work out just right
But to have a good attitude will help it turn out alright

__Rose__ - Rose is typically made from the same grapes used to make red wine. The kinds of red grapes used to create rose often vary; it can be one kind of grape or a variety. Roses are known for their light pink color, which can be achieved a number of ways, usually before the grape juice is even fermented into wine.

In the face of adversity, teach to stay positive and upbeat
So they will not feel like giving up, even though they may face defeat

When you can see the positive in a situation
It will prove to serve you much better in the long run
People gravitate to those that seem happy & fun
Not someone that just throws in the towel & is done

Life can sometimes be certainly no picnic
The best you can do is be optimistic

The alternative is to commiserate & stew
On all of the things that don't seem to go right for you
Is that really how you want people to look at you?

You want others to see you as someone that's carefree
They tend to gravitate to people that seem happy
Not to those that are down & wallow in self pity

So teach your kids to hang on, because through it they will pull
Be positive, so the (wine) glass will always be half full

LESSON 10

QUE SYRAH, SYRAH...WHAT WILL BE, WILL BE!

In the end, you simply can't control and perfect it all
You and your kid are going to figuratively fall

You are both going to make mistakes all along the way
And you each need to know that, and that it will be okay
It's what you do with those lessons at the end of the day

The important thing is how you both use lessons to grow
It will teach you strength, resilience and the power to know
That next time you can catch the curveballs that life tends to throw

---

***Syrah** or Shiraz is a dark-skinned grape grown throughout the world and used primarily to produce powerful red wines. Whether sold as Syrah or Shiraz, these wines enjoy great popularity.*

***Champagne Cup** – A punch containing a sparkling wine*

***Chablis** - dry white table wine of Chablis, France or a wine resembling it*

Sometimes you just have to accept things as they happen, because one never knows
You can't predict when a hit comes your way or when it throws you some major blows

Be malleable as life throws punches at you
Doing so will only help you to keep plowing through

If you fall, it's ok….brush yourself off and get back up
And pour yourself a nice sparkling punch in a ***champagne cup***

Or enjoy the ride with a nice glass of ***Chablis***
And say…Que **Syrah, Syrah**…what will be, will be

LESSON 11:

CORKED

In the end, you sometimes just get a bad grape in the bunch!

Just kidding......kids don't come out of the womb "corked" or knowing hate, prejudice, bad behavior, etc...they are a blank canvas when they are born, just like a seed that is planted to become a grape that will later be turned into a wine. For the seed to turn into a grape good enough to be made into a wine, a lot of care is put into growing the grape. There is a lot of thought that goes into how the seed grows....the environment (ie the weather, the soil), how it is cared for while growing, how it is picked once mature, etc. The same holds true for children...they are a blank canvas when they are born and how they are raised shapes how they become. They become the product of their learned behavior and how you raise them. They are so impressionable...more than more parents realize, and adapt learned behaviors from what they see and hear in addition to what you teach so if you are teaching one lesson but displaying another behavior they learn that, too. The point is....parenting is hard but you have the power and responsibility to shape your child as a good person. Hopefully this book showed you that you shouldn't feel badly when you feel overwhelmed and just want to dive into a bottle of wine and give up. It's okay and you should enjoy that glass but also be inspired by that glass to raise your kids the right way!

Corked - *A corked wine is not one with bits of cork floating in it. It's a tasting term used to describe wines contaminated by a chemical compound that is the product of mold infection in the cork. Said to affect 5% of bottles, it is one of the main reasons behind the drive towards the increasing use of screw caps and synthetic closures. It may result in a wine that simply lacks fruit and can be difficult to spot, or it may be horribly obvious, with a cardboard, musty, mushroomy taste with dank aromas and flavors, rendering the wine completely undrinkable and faulty. This is one of the main reasons at a restaurant that the server will open the wine and have you taste it before pouring you a full glass.*

A Basic understanding of how wine is made:

Viticulture: cultivation of grapes and grape vines. The taste of the wine is based on the kind of grapes used. The taste of grapes differs on many factors (the place where they are grown, the climate (humidity of the region is a big factor), quality of the soil, the drainage system, exposure to the sun, etc).

Harvesting: The next step after cultivation is harvesting. Harvesting of the finely cultivated grapes is very important. Knowing the precise timing of taking the grapes off the fine takes experience. The grapes need to be at their optimal prime and ripped to the right combination of sugar, acid and moisture. The harvesting of the grapes can be done in two ways either by manually or mechanically. However, most of the wineries follow manual method, as it is a more hands on method to ensure only the optimal grapes are picked and bad grapes don't get through (as they sometimes do in mechanical methods).

Pressing and Crushing: Here the grapes are first pressed and then crushed so that their inherent flavor is got in the form of liquid. Most of the wineries use specialized machines for this crushing process. The liquid that is formed after crushing and pressing the grapes is referred to as must. At this stage the wine will either turn its color into red or white depending on the choice of the winemaker. The liquid turns red when they are just left aside after the crushing step. So if you want red color leave the must for a certain period of time after crushing. If you want white color then to separate the skin after pressing step, the must become white.

Fermentation: Grapes easily get fermented since they have a good quantity of sugar and moisture that reacts with the wild yeast. Fermentation period is on average between 10 to 30 days; however the period of fermentation depends on the quality of grapes and the climate.

Stabilization: Here the unwanted substance is removed before bottling so that they won't cause muddle or crystal formation in the finished wine.

Bottling: This the final stage where the clarified solution is transferred in the wooden barrels or bottles

WINE